Green Bible Stories for Children

Green Bible Stories for Children

Tami Lehman-Wilzig

illustrations by
Durga Yael Bernhard

KAR-BEN
PUBLISHING

To my grandson Alon Amiel. May you grow up with an
eco-love of nature and equal love of the Bible.

Special thanks to Rachel Oser, a most accomplished woman:
Mother, Rabbanit, Science Teacher & On-Line Science Education Specialist,
who provided invaluable guidance for all the story activities.
— T.L.W.

For Rabbi Jonathan Kligler, with all my appreciation.
— D.Y.B.

Text copyright © 2011 by Tami Lehman-Wilzig
Illustrations copyright © 2011 by Durga Yael Bernhard
The image in this book is used with the permission of: © iStockphoto.com/Bill Noll, (all backgrounds).

Kar-Ben Publishing
A division of Lerner Publishing Group, Inc.
241 First Avenue North
Minneapolis, Minnesota 55401 U.S.A.
800-4KARBEN

Website address: www.karben.com

Library of Congress Cataloging-in-Publication Data

Lehman-Wilzig, Tami.
    Green Bible stories for children/ by Tami Lehman-Wilzig ; illustrations by Durga Yael Bernhard.
      p.   cm.
    ISBN 978-0-7613-5135-1 (lib. bdg. : alk. paper)
    1. Nature—Religious aspects—Judaism—Juvenile literature. 2. Human ecology—Religious
aspects—Judaism—Juvenile literature. 3. Bible stories, English—O.T. I. Bernhard, Durga. II. Title.
  BS1199.N34L44 2011
  220.8'3337—dc22   2009031516

Manufactured in the United States of America
1 – CG – 7/15/2011

JUNE 2013

Contents

In the Beginning...

....we had a perfectly planned planet. Creating the world didn't happen right away. God had a master plan with something new each day:

Day 1: Night and Day came our way.

Day 2: Then there appeared a sky so high.

Day 3: To balance the heavens, plants, trees, and grass shot up down below.

Day 4: The sun, moon, and stars came into being, leading to different seasons.

Day 5: Large bodies of water floated into the picture, home to different schools of fish.

Day 6: Families of every four-legged creature established their natural habitats. Feeling something was missing, God created a two-legged person to rule the planet and gave him a mate and a mandate: *"Be fruitful and multiply. Let the land benefit you. Be wise and use it carefully."*

Day 7: Tired after all this work, God decided it was time to rest and created Shabbat—the day of rest.

Unfortunately, when all was done, everything started to go wrong. Man and woman didn't obey God. By the time Noah appeared, God was disgusted with the behavior of mankind and decided that it was time to start anew.

Noah is the first of several "green" Bible stories that illustrate the book's concern with the environment. In tale after tale, the Bible gives a blueprint for how to preserve planet earth. As you read these stories and discover how you can make your world more eco-friendly, you'll understand how the Bible planted the seeds of environmental concern.

Variety is the Spice of Life
Noah's Ark

An ecosystem is made up of a variety of plants, animals, and micro-organisms all working together. The preservation of these species is the message of Noah's Ark. Following God's instructions, Noah collected pairs of each type of animal, bird, and insect onto his ark. While creepy crawlers may bug you, and you may find some animals beastly, always remember that to save our planet, "the more the merrier" is usually true.

Generations after Adam and Eve, God took a good look at his planet and frowned. "Everyone is misbehaving. It's time to give the earth a fresh start."

The question was how. Flooded with ideas, God realized *that* was the answer. "To heal this land I have to wash it out completely."

Still, God did not want to redo all the hard work of creation. Looking around, God found one good man named Noah. "Why endanger Noah and all the species I have created?" God asked.

After much thought, God came up with a plan and whispered to Noah, "Psst, Noah. I need your help. You and your family are the only good people around. Everyone else has ruined the earth. You can help me heal it and repopulate it."

"Me? How?" asked Noah.

"It's simple," continued God. "Your

talented hands already plant and plow. Now I'm going to teach you how to build."

"A house?" asked Noah.

"A house boat," corrected God. "You are going to become the builder and captain of the first ocean liner. I have the measurements. All you have to do is follow directions."

Noah listened. "This is a tall order for our narrow rivers and small lakes," he commented.

"Did you ever hear of a flood?" asked God.

Noah shook his head.

"You will soon. You'll hear the storm. Huge rains will make the rivers rise. But you and your family will be safe."

"All by ourselves?" Noah's voice quivered.

"Of course not," assured God. "I will always be by your side. Plus, you're going to have passengers. I want you to take two of every type of beast, bird, and insect with you. Don't worry about the fish. They know how to swim."

So Noah did as God commanded. With the help of his sons, he built a three-story ark. He set aside separate areas for food and waste matter, to safeguard the health of man and beast.

After 40 days of steady rain, the ark sailed high on the waters, as the earth sank out of sight. After several months, Noah steered the ark to the top of Mt. Ararat, waiting for the waters to recede. He sent out a raven to scout for dry land, but the bird returned empty-beaked. So he sent out a dove, who also returned with wet feet. The next dove returned with an olive leaf, and the third did not return. It was time for Noah and his family to leave the ark. God created a rainbow of dazzling colors, promising never again to flood the land. Once again, earth was in mankind's hands.

Become a Biodiversity Detective

You don't have to board Noah's Ark to see the diversity in the natural world. Just step into your own backyard.

What you need:
Notebook and pencil
Magnifying glass
Tape measure
String
Seeds
Gardening tools

- Step out into your backyard or go to a nearby park. Section off an area about two feet square and mark it off with string.
- Using the magnifying glass, see how many species you can identify. Look for grass, flowers, bushes, insects, worms, and even fungus. Record them in your notebook.
- Go to a local nursery and buy seeds for one or two native plants. Plant them and follow growing instructions on the packets.
- Once the seeds sprout, get out your magnifying glass and count how many species you see. Is there a change in the area's biodiversity?
- Record all the species in your notebook, and compare "Before" and "After" you planted the seeds.

Check Out Biodiversity at the Zoo

The animals on Noah's Ark may have been on the world's first cruise, but they were caged in. In the past, zoos continued Noah's tradition of putting animals in pens, but today most zoos are "open." Visit an open zoo and ask a zookeeper:

- Are different animals paired in the same habitats?
- What and when do they eat? Do they graze or are they given only animal feed?
- Take a sketch pad with you and draw an open habitat. Make sure you pencil in all the details: animals, insects, birds, feeding spots, trees, shrubbery, etc.

Now visit a petting zoo. Compare and record the differences in the two zoo environments:

- How much space do the animals have?
- Do they graze, or are they given only animal feed?
- Are the insects different from the ones at the open zoo?
- Are birds flying freely or housed in cages?
- Count and compare the different types of creatures in the two zoos.
- Take out your sketch pad and draw the differences. Hint: Don't forget to draw yourself at the petting zoo!

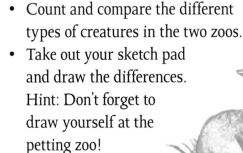

Greener Pastures
Abraham and Sustainable Herding

The Jewish people started out as a nation of herders. Like all good herdsmen, Abraham understood that because the land and its nutrients must constantly be renewed, herds must give it a rest by moving on to forage in new fields.

Abraham was a man on the move. At God's command, he gathered his wife, his nephew Lot, and all his possessions, and left Haran, his birthplace.

When they reached Canaan, God called out to Abraham, "Look at the territory before you. It is my gift to your offspring."

When food became scarce, Abraham moved the family again, this time to Egypt, where he and Lot became wealthy men. Once they had amassed enough cattle, silver, and gold, they returned to Canaan.

Back in their homeland, Abraham saw that the amount of livestock he and Lot owned was too much for grazing on one parcel of land. Family feuds began.

"Our cattle got here first!" Lot's shepherds shouted.

"These are our pastures," insisted Abraham's herdsmen.

"This can't continue," said Abraham.

Turning to Lot, he said, "Your herd is overgrazing and not allowing the earth to renew itself. The cattle chew away the vegetation, and without plant life, the soil cannot absorb enough of the sun's rays. The new plants will be weaker and soon only weeds will grow. The land will become a desert, leaving nothing for the cattle to eat.

"We can't afford to ruin the source of our livelihood," continued Abraham. "There is more land in this country beyond these patches. It's time we each went our own way. Choose which land you want, and I'll take my household in the opposite direction."

Lot became an urban dweller, pitching his tents as far away as Sodom. A lover of the land, Abraham chose a more modest way of life, making sure to safeguard all that nature had to offer.

Create A "Carrying Capacity" Collage

Carrying capacity is the term used for how many animals a given area can accommodate. It's like asking if a one-bedroom house would be big enough for two parents and six kids.

What you need:
White and colored construction paper
Scissors, pencils, markers, paste

- Cut out meadows, grass, trees, and fences and paste them on a sheet of 8 ½" x 11" paper to make a grazing pasture.
- Now draw and cut out 20 cows about 2" square and start pasting. Is there enough room in your pasture to accommodate all of them?
- Now make a bird cage collage. Draw a large cage on an 8 ½" x 11" piece of paper.
- Then draw, cut out and paste down gravel, a feeder, a cup for water, a swing, and a perch.
- Now ask yourself how many parakeets will fit in a cage this size with enough room to fly around, eat, and drink.

A Whale of a Time

There's nothing fishy about going to an aquarium. What's really cool is watching the whales. But to keep whales in captivity, their tanks must be huge. Ask one of the guides to explain about a tank's carrying capacity, and have a whale of a time finding out how these animals eat, sleep, and communicate.

Preventing Famine
Joseph Plans Ahead

Unfortunately we can't control Mother Nature. We can't prevent earthquakes, tsunamis, volcanic eruptions, and droughts. However, we can plan for them. Joseph had the wisdom to prevent disaster when he knew a drought was imminent.

One night Pharaoh, King of Egypt, had two frightening dreams. Waking up, he commanded, "Bring me Egypt's best magicians and wise men. I need these dreams interpreted.

"In my first dream," Pharaoh said, "seven fat cows rose out of the river. While they were feeding, seven starving cows rose up and devoured the fat ones, but they remained skinny."

"Holy cow!" exclaimed one of the magicians.

Pharaoh continued, "In my second dream, seven full ears of corn cropped up, only to be stalked and eaten by seven thin ears."

"We could give you answers," said king's advisors, "but the truth is we don't have a clue."

"Wait a minute," interrupted Pharaoh's chief cupbearer. "I know just the guy for you. When the baker and I were in prison we had some strange dreams also. An inmate named Joseph explained them, and everything he predicted came true!"

"Bring me Joseph now!" commanded Pharaoh.

Joseph was quickly brought from the jail. He listened to Pharaoh's dreams and asked: "What do you want first, the good news or the bad news?"

"I want the truth," growled Pharaoh.

"I wouldn't dream of telling you lies," answered Joseph. He then explained that both dreams predicted seven years of plenty followed by seven years of famine.

"What you've got to do now," advised Joseph, "is appoint someone to plan for Egypt's future. During these next seven good years, he will have to oversee a program to store food. That way, when the crops fail, no one will starve."

"Brilliant!" declared Pharaoh, adding, "You're my man! If you can interpret my dreams, you can do the job."

For the next seven years, Joseph gathered grain and corn and stored it in the cities. When the famine hit, Joseph opened up the storehouses, rationing the saved provisions. His foresight saved the Egyptians from starvation.

Create Your Own Survival Kit

Joseph prepared for seven years of food shortages. All of us should be prepared for emergencies. Put together your own, one-day survival kit and encourage your family members to do the same.

You will need:

Sturdy plastic storage box with cover

Box of dry cereal

Package of powdered milk

8-pack of bottled water

Empty plastic bottle for making milk

Jar of peanut butter

Granola bars

Plastic bowls and silverware

Paper towels and/or moist towelettes

Portable radio and extra batteries

Flashlight with extra batteries

Books and puzzles

In A Pickle

Historically, pickling was a way to preserve food for times when fresh vegetables weren't available. Try it yourself with cucumbers.

You will need:

Clean half gallon jar

1-2 lb. pickling cucumbers, washed and dried

Bunch of fresh dill

6 cloves garlic, peeled

1 c. kosher salt dissolved in 2 quarts of water

2 packets of pickling spices tied in cheese cloth (about 2 Tbsp. each)

1. Place half the dill, half the garlic, and one of the spice packets on the bottom of the jar.
2. Place the cucumbers inside the jar and fill with salt water until not quite full.
3. Add the other packet of pickling spices and the remaining garlic and dill on the top.
4. Seal the jar and place in a cool place. In a week, foam will start to form as the pickles begin to sour. The longer they sit the more sour they will taste.

Natural Pest Control Tips

Michal Mazaki, an agronomist at Agrexco, Israel's largest agricultural exporter, specializes in pest control. She offers these tips to help keep pests from your plants:

- Throw out sick plants to prevent the spread of disease.
- Remove insects by hand, using disposable gloves.
- If you see holes on the leaves, give your plant a good shake. Wait 20 seconds, then look for caterpillars under the plant and get rid of them.
- Cover your plants with nets that let in the sun, but keep out the bugs.
- Collect ladybugs to put inside the net. They protect plants by eating up pests.
- Add liquid soap to a cup of water to create home-made bug spray.

Joseph and those Pesky Pests

What did Joseph do to keep pests from the grain he stored? Israeli archaeologists found the remains of a beetle in a grain of wheat dug up in an ancient Beit She'an granary. They think it dates back to the time of Joseph. The Biblical commentator Rashi suggests that fine grains of sand were sprinkled among the wheat to prevent it from going bad. The sand would scratch the beetle's hard shell, causing it to dry up and die.

Sweet Water From a Tree
Moses in the Desert

Today, one of the world's major ecological concerns is the shortage of drinking water. Israel is a good example of a modern country with very little usable water. That's why it is developing new ways to remove salt from sea water, in order to make the water drinkable. Long ago, Moses discovered that desalination is an effective way to create drinkable water in a desert environment. The story of Moses using a tree branch to sweeten the water is thought to be a miracle, but Australian researchers have found that specific trees do reduce the salt level of water!

After Moses led the Children of Israel out of Egypt, they found themselves in the wilderness of Shur.

"This *sure* is rough living," the people complained to Moses. "We're thirsty. You didn't tell us to take water jugs, and there's not a stream in sight."

Moses kept on trekking. The Israelites

followed. Soon they came upon a brook. The people eagerly tasted the water, but immediately spat it out.

"It's bitter," they complained. "We can't drink this."

"Help us!" Moses cried to God. "Your people are dying of thirst."

"O.K.," agreed God. "I'm going to give you a lesson on how to manage the land and its resources. You see that tree over there? I want you to cut it down and throw its branches into the water. The natural properties of that tree will make the brackish water sweet."

Moses did as God commanded. After a while, the water tasted as refreshing as a natural spring. The Israelites drank and quenched their thirst.

"We never realized how precious fresh water is," they said to Moses.

They continued their journey, and when they reached Elim, they found 12 water springs and rows of lush palm trees.

"A garden in the desert? How can this be?" the people wondered.

"It's called an oasis." Moses answered. "God is showing us that as long as there is water, trees and plants can grow even in the driest climate. God has given us this gift, but it's up to us to learn how to properly manage our water resources."

The Children of Israel realized that Elim would be a good place to set up camp, stock up on clean, safe water, and let their livestock drink before continuing their journey.

Salt Water to Fresh Water

Every Passover we make saltwater to remind us of the tears the Children of Israel cried while they were slaves. Now let's celebrate their freedom by desalinating the water:

- Stir 2 Tbsp. of salt into 2 cups of water. Take a sip and observe the taste.
- Pour the water into a bowl and place a small glass in the middle. Cover the bowl tightly with plastic wrap.
- Place a quarter coin in the middle of the tight wrap. The plastic wrap in the center will now sag.
- Place the bowl in the sun for 3-4 hours. The water will evaporate, leaving the salt behind, and the vapor will rise to the top of the wrap.
- Droplets will form and drop into the cup as the water condenses.
- After 4 hours, remove the plastic wrap and taste the water that has accumulated in the glass. How does this compare to the taste of the saltwater you made?

Harvesting the Salt

During Biblical times the Children of Israel harvested salt by pouring seawater into pits and letting the water evaporate. Perhaps they went to the waters of the Dead Sea, one of the world's saltiest bodies of water with a 33.7% salt level. The next time you're near the ocean, try harvesting salt:

- Fill a glass jar with seawater and add an additional 1/3 cup of salt.
- Let the jar stand uncovered for 15 minutes. Some of the salt will sink to the bottom.
- Pour the clear water into another jar, making sure the settled salt stays at the bottom of the first jar.
- Put jar with clear water outdoors in the sun for several days.
- Foam will begin to form on the water's surface as it evaporates and fine salt crystals begin to form.
- In a few days, the water level will go down, and salt crystals will attach themselves to the inside of the jar.
- Once you see enough salt coating the inside of the jar, it's ready to be scraped off. It's safe to eat, but best not to do so since it's been sitting outdoors unattended.

Reduce, Reuse, Recycle
Building the Tabernacle

In "eco" terms, recycling is one of the three "R"s: Reduce, Reuse, Recycle. Recycling decreases waste and reduces pollution. You can reduce waste by reusing materials and recycling them into new products. The very first recycling lesson is found in the Bible, when the Israelites were instructed to build the *mishkan*, a tabernacle for the Holy Ark.

"I want my tablets to be housed in a sacred space with sacred furnishings," God said, when he gave the Ten Commandments to the Israelites.

"Where will we find the materials in this wilderness?" Moses asked.

"Have you forgotten the precious metals and beautiful fabrics you received from the Egyptians when you left Egypt? The Israelites can practice their first lesson in Recycling. They can Reuse the jewels and metals by melting them down and turning them into candlesticks and ritual breastplates."

"And the textiles?" asked Moses.

"Another lesson in Resourcefulness. They will unravel the cloth, spin, weave, dye, and Reuse it."

Seeing that Moses reacted with interest, God continued, "In my oceans there are different shellfish that wash onto the shore. Even though they can't be eaten, they are the source of special dark blue, violet, and red dyes—the majestic colors my children will need to dye the fabrics for my tabernacle."

Moses began visualizing the *mishkan*— with different rooms inside for praying and showing devotion. That meant a lot of interior decorating. Somehow he had a feeling that God would enumerate which materials could be used for these new purposes. He grabbed a large flat stone and an etching stick.

"I'm all ears," he announced, waiting for the list. And sure enough the instructions came down from on high—all of which are recorded in Exodus 25: 1–7.

Make Your Own Toy Road System

Instead of going to the toy store for something new, create toys from recycled materials.

Collect empty cartons, cardboard, and cereal boxes. Tape the flattened cartons and cardboard together to make a large road system. Next get to work drawing streets, parks, and lakes.

- Use empty match boxes to create cars and trucks.
- Use buttons for their wheels.
- Turn empty paper towel rolls into tunnels.
- Connect toilet paper rolls to make a curved bridge.
- Use clean, recycled cans for factories and skyscrapers.

Make Your Own Dollhouse

Collect cartons of various sizes with inner partitions. Connect them together to make a one- or two-story house. Use the partitions for your rooms. Don't worry about cutting a few apart in order to expand the room—that's what renovation is all about. Now it's time to furnish and decorate:

- Recycle gift wrap and use it for wallpaper.
- Place wine corks under match boxes for tables. Cut up fancy napkins for tablecloths.
- Use small gift boxes for beds and chairs.
- Use broken jewelry and beads to make lamps and other accessories.

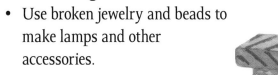

Every Seven Years
A Sabbath for the Land

Farmers practicing sustainable agriculture cooperate with nature. They understand that they cannot plant more crops than the land can handle. Crop rotation—planting different crops at different times in the same field—is one way to ensure that the earth is not overworked. The "Shmita Year," a year-long rest from planting, was the Bible's way of maintaining sustainable agriculture. It allowed the earth to renew itself and stock up on nutrients necessary for future crop yields.

One day God told Moses, "I've decided that the Sabbath is not only for humans. I've taken a good look at the land and how hard it works. I think it deserves a sabbatical—a year off to renew itself."

"What do you suggest?" Moses asked.

"For one full year there will be no picking, no pruning, no plowing, to allow the earth to replenish its energy," God explained.

"When?" asked Moses.

"Well, seven is my favorite number. Every seventh year they will let the earth rest. It will be the *Shmita Year,* the Sabbath for the land."

Moses looked to the heavens, imploring: "How will the people eat? You know how they love to complain."

"It's okay to pick and eat fruit that grows on its own, such as berries, as well as plants that grow wild," God continued. "You may water, fertilize, weed, and spray existing plants and trees. And the poor may eat from the leavings of the fields.

"People need to learn to store and save when the crops are bountiful, so they'll have enough for themselves and their animals during the year of rest."

And so the Shmita Year came into being. People understood that the earth needs to rest.

The Effects of Overcrowding

Sustainable farming is rooted in Shmita, but you can always check to see if your plants have enough "breathing space."

- Save tangerine seeds in a small, moistened plastic bag.
- Fill 6 clean, dry yogurt containers half way with fresh potting soil.
- Plant a tangerine seed in each container, then water the plants.
- Arrange the containers in 2 rows of 3 each.
- For the first week, water when the soil feels dry. Don't overwater.
- Once plants begin to sprout, plant another seed in one row of containers and continue to water all of them.
- At the end of the second week, plant a third tangerine seed in the same row of containers and continue to water all of them.
- At the end of the third week, compare the quality of the plants in the containers that have 3 seeds to those with only 1 seed. Is there a difference in the way they stand? The width of the stems? The size of the leaves? Which look healthier?

Food Storage Experiment: Dry Your Own Apricots

Part of observing Shmita is to learn how to store and save food for the time when there will be no yield. Drying fruit is a good example. The best time to try this experiment is in the summer, when the sun is strong.

- Dissolve a Vitamin C tablet in a glass of water.
- Wash 4 apricots, cut them in half, and remove the pits. Place them on a wire rack and sprinkle them with some Vitamin C water.
- Cover the rack with netting and place it in the sun. Bring it inside each night so that the apricot halves won't get wet with dew.
- Check them daily. Once the halves have dried on one side (after 2 to 4 days), turn them over and sprinkle the other side with the vitamin water.
- When the apricots are fully dried, taste one. Store the rest in a plastic bag in a cool, dry place.
- After a week, taste them again. Are they still good?

With a Mighty Sound
Joshua Destroys Jericho

Sound affects the environment, making noise pollution a major ecological problem. Loud blasts can create stress in animals, leading to abnormal behavior and possible extinction. Similarly, the racket of traffic, the roar of a jet plane, or any other loud, hammering sound can permanently damage a person's hearing and affect their well-being. As Joshua discovered, it also can severely damage a city's infrastructure.

Shortly before his death, Moses chose Joshua to succeed him as the leader of the Israelites.

Joshua's task was to conquer the land called Canaan. His first battle would be at Jericho, a heavily-armed town west of the Jordan River. God's plan was for Joshua to use noise to cause the destruction. The sound would be so loud that it would crack the ramparts and collapse the city's walls.

Joshua understood the power of noise. He had been at Mt. Sinai and remembered the loud shofar blast that came out of the thick cloud. He had witnessed how the Israelites

trembled. But to make a city's walls fall apart?

When Joshua brought his army to Jericho, the walls were tightly sealed. No one could go in or out.

God commanded Joshua, "March your soldiers quietly around the city walls once a day for the next six days."

"Soldiers don't walk softly," countered Joshua.

"They will this time," God insisted. "You're going to use the sounds of silence as a surprise tactic." Pausing, God added, "You'll also need seven priests carrying trumpets made out of ram's horns. Station them in front of the Holy Ark."

"Am I going to use them as surround sound?" Joshua asked.

"Eventually," replied God. "But we are going to keep their mouths as tightly shut as Jericho's walls for the first six days."

Joshua did as instructed. And on the seventh day, God changed the tempo.

"Blast those trumpets and have all the people shout at once," God commanded. "Then witness what noise can do to a city's surroundings."

Joshua didn't have to wait long to observe the power of high decibels. The walls of Jericho came tumbling down, allowing his army to enter the city and capture it easily.

How Does Your Garden Grow?

Loud music can cause noise pollution. Let's see if this has an effect on nature.

- Place 2 identical plants each in a separate room and make sure each receives the same amount of sunlight, water, and plant food.
- For 1-2 hours each day, play soothing classical music next to one plant, and hard rock next to the other. Make sure the plants can't hear each other's music.
- At the end of a week, check the health and growth of each plant. Is one flourishing while the other one is drooping? Maybe you'll see other differences as well.

What's All The Buzz About?

- Catch a few of the same kind of insects and put them in a covered, plastic jar. Punch small holes in the lid to allow them to breathe. Observe how they move around in the jar.
- Now play some rock music near the jar and see if the insects are attracted or repelled by the noise.
- Give your insects a 15-minute break, then try the same procedure with classical music. How do they behave now?
- Give the insects another 15-minute break. Now observe their behavior again. Is it the same as it was before you played any of the music, or has their behavior been altered by hearing music?
- Return your insects to their natural habitat.

Solar Power
Joshua Harnesses the Sun

The importance of sunlight is recorded in the Bible when Joshua realized that he needed additional daylight for his battle strategy. Today, we're harnessing the sun's rays to save energy: skylights help reduce the use of electricity; solar panels heat water; greenhouses convert the sun's light into heat; and solar electric hybrid vehicles may well be the wave of the future.

Joshua was on the march. He had conquered the cities of Ai and Jericho, and signed a peace treaty with the people of Gibeon. But the neighboring kingdoms were not pleased. Fearing Gibeon's increased power, they massed armies at its borders. The people of Gibeon asked Joshua and his army to help defend them.

Joshua quickly gathered his brave fighters and, with God's assurance, they marched toward the city. The enemy scattered in confusion as hailstones rained down on them. But Joshua needed more time.

"I don't want this battle going into overtime," he told God. "It started today and I want it to end today. I need more daylight. The sun is my secret weapon."

Knowing God was on his side, Joshua looked up at the sky and commanded, "Listen to me, sun. Stay where you are, shining over Gibeon. And moon, you stay in the Valley of Ayalon for just a bit longer."

And so the sun stood still, adding a few hours to the day, until Joshua and his army were victorious.

Calculate the Sun's Power

The sun is a renewable source of energy. To see the sun in action, compare the performance of a solar-powered calculator versus a battery-operated calculator.

- Place the solar-powered calculator near a window and the battery-powered calculator on your desk.
- Charge your solar calculator according to package directions. Turn on your battery-powered calculator. Use both calculators for the rest of the day.
- If the solar calculator gets weak when the sun goes down, place it under a light source.
- Keep a log and count how many days it takes for the battery-powered calculator to stop working. Then check the performance of your solar-powered calculator. You will see that the sun is the true energizer!

Check Your Electric Meter

Daylight Savings Time is designed to help us save energy. For a full week before Daylight Savings Time goes into effect, check your electric meter and keep a log of usage. Do the same thing for a full week after you change the clocks. Compare the results. Does the extra hour of sunlight help your family save on electricity?

How should people relate to nature? The laws and practices of the Bible have much to say.

Bal Tashchit: Don't Waste or Destroy

When in your war against a city you have to besiege it a long time in order to capture it, you must not destroy its trees...
You may eat of them, but you must not cut them down...
Only trees that you know do not yield food may be destroyed.
Deuteronomy 20: 19-20

The average person produces over four pounds of waste every day! We throw away food, discard things that can be recycled, and pollute our rivers and streams with garbage. Long ago, the Children of Israel learned not to misuse the land, even when they were at war. The Biblical law of *Bal Tashchit* (Do Not Destroy) taught them how to preserve the environment. Over the centuries, the rabbis have expanded the principle of Bal Tashchit. They have taught us to use only what is necessary in its simplest and least expensive form.

Tza'ar Ba'alei Chayim: Prevent Animal Suffering

Remember the Sabbath day and keep it holy. Six days you shall labor and do all your work, but the seventh day is a Sabbath of the Lord your God; you shall not do any work — you, your son or daughter, your male or female slave, or your cattle, or the stranger who is within your settlements.
Exodus 20:10

Americans have been celebrating "Be Kind to Animals Week" in the month of May since 1915, but this precept goes as far back as the Ten Commandments. The Sabbath Day is not only for people, but for animals as well.

Other laws instruct us to:

- Return a lost animal to its rightful owner (Exodus 23:5)
- Send a mother bird away before taking her eggs (Deuteronomy 22: 6–7)
- Make life as comfortable as possible for work animals (Deuteronomy 25: 4)

Keep the Environment Clean

. . . there shall be an area for you outside the camp, where you may relieve yourself. With your gear you shall have a spike, and when you have squatted you shall dig a hole with it and cover up your excrement.
Deuteronomy 23:13-14

You've seen these signs everywhere: *Keep Your City Clean, Don't Trash Our Beaches, Use Your Pooper Scooper*. Even in Biblical times, keeping the environment clean and pollution-free was a priority. That's why in the book of Deuteronomy the Israelites are commanded to dispose of their waste by burying it in the ground, not by throwing it into a nearby river or littering the countryside.

Orlah: Letting Trees Mature

When you . . . plant any tree for food . . . three years it (the fruit) shall be forbidden for you, not to be eaten. In the fourth year, all its fruit shall be set aside for jubilation . . . And only in the fifth year, may you use its fruit — that its yield to you may be increased.
Leviticus 19:23

The Bible was early to note that plants need time to mature. For this reason, it forbids us to eat from fruit trees for the first three years. (*Laws of Orlah*). Fruit from the fourth year may be consumed at celebrations, and fruit from the fifth year on is for public consumption.

Urban Planning

Instruct the Israelite people to assign . . . towns for the Levites to dwell in; you shall also assign pasture land around their towns. The towns shall be theirs to dwell in, and the pasture shall be for the cattle they own and all their other beasts . . . The town pasture . . . shall extend 1,000 cubits outside the town wall all around . . .
Numbers 35:2–4

Urban planning is rooted in a Biblical command. The Israelite tribes are instructed as to how much land should be set aside for pasture and open space. The Biblical commentator Rashi interpreted this command as one designed to protect the beauty and ecological health of the city.

Roots of a Vegetarian Diet

God said, "See, I give you every seed-bearing plant that is upon all the earth, and every tree that has seed-bearing fruit; they shall be yours for food."
Genesis 1: 29

Although the Bible does not require us to become vegetarians, many who opt for a vegetarian diet find support in it. They note that when Adam is introduced to the Garden of Eden, he is offered only the fruits and vegetables that God created. Vegetarians also cite the Bible's compassion towards animals.

Counting the Blessings of Nature

Ancient Israel was a nation of farmers—growers and herdsmen. That's why many Jewish holidays revolve around planting and harvesting crops. The rabbis understood that water is the key to successful farming, and that one must go with the flow of nature's cycles. They created many prayers acknowledging nature's role.

- **Rain:** On *Shemini Atzeret*, following the harvest holiday of *Sukkot*, a prayer for rain is recited. In addition, during Israel's rainy season (from early December until Passover), a line asking for rain is inserted in the daily *Shemonah Esrei* prayer.

- **Dew:** After Passover, there is no rainfall in Israel. The rabbis understood that the land still needs moisture and added a prayer for dew, to be recited on the first day of Passover.

- **Cycles of nature:** Blessings are recited 1) over the first blossoming fruit trees in spring, 2) the first time a new fruit is eaten each season, and 3) every 28 years, when, according to Jewish tradition, the sun is positioned as it was at creation.

- **Food and Drink:** Blessings are recited before and after eating.

Shavuot

The first food drive is recorded in the Bible. When we read the book of *Ruth* on the holiday of Shavuot, we learn about the kindness of Boaz. He knows not to waste the grain that his workers have overlooked, and allows Ruth to reap the leftover bounty of his field.

Tu B'Shevat: The Jewish Arbor Day

This New Year for Trees was first referred to in the *Mishnah*, a commentary on the Torah. The rabbis created the holiday as a way of determining the age of fruit trees. The *Kabbalists* (Jewish mystics), created a *Tu B'Shevat* seder that celebrates the variety of fruits and nuts. In Israel *Tu B'Shevat* is an occasion to plant trees to symbolize the rebirth of the Jewish homeland. Israel's growing forests have had important ecological benefits: increased rainfall, less soil erosion, and fewer desert areas.

About the Author and Illustrator

Tami Lehman-Wilzig has a Bachelor's Degree in English Literature and a Master's Degree in Communications from Boston University. She is one of Israel's leading English language copywriters. Her children's books include *Tasty Bible Stories, Keeping the Promise, Passover Around the World, Hanukkah Around the World,* and *Zvuvi's Israel.* She lives in Petach Tikvah, Israel.

Durga Yael Bernhard was raised in New York's Hudson Valley and began painting at the age of 13. She studied at the Art Students' League of New York, the School of Visual Arts, and SUNY Purchase. She is the illustrator of many children's books, including fiction and non-fiction, natural science titles, and multicultural folktales. She lives in the Catskill Mountains of New York.